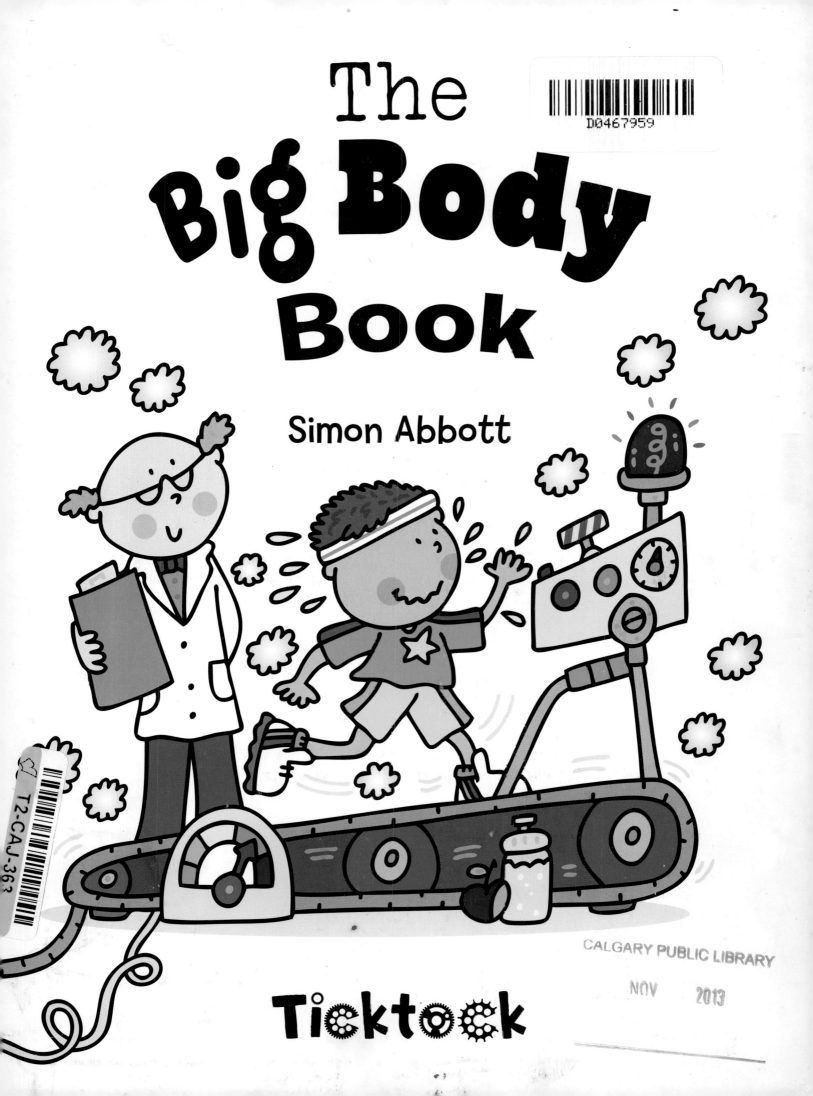

The Big Body Book

Simon Abbott

Ticktock

Your Amazing Body

Your body is amazing and it is always hard at work.
It is busy doing millions of things while you are reading
this page. Let's see what's happening....

Blood is racing through your
arteries and **veins**, carrying
everything your body
needs to keep going.

New cells are being made -
every second your body makes
about 2 million blood cells.

Liver

Kidney

It takes food between 24-36 hours
to travel from your mouth,
through your **intestines,**
and out the other end!

Your **nails** are growing at
around one-tenth of an inch
(3 mm) every month.

Pee is trickling into your **bladder.**
You will really need to empty it by the
time it's about three-quarters full.

Your **hair** is growing at about half an inch (12 mm) every month.

Lung

Your **heart** is beating at about 85 times per minute.

Stomach

Move it!

Inside your body, there is a tough frame of hard bones called your skeleton. Without it, you'd be a blubbery bag of jelly! Your muscles hook on to your bones and make them move.

When you walk, jump, and run, it is your **muscles** that do the work.

Your muscles are like sets of ropes. They work in **pairs** by pulling on your skeleton to move your bones.

Pulls to straighten leg

Pulls to bend leg

Your body has about **650** separate muscles.

Your bones are **bendy** so they're less likely to break.

Bones are as hard as granite when squeezed and four times stronger than concrete when stretched.

Broken bones can mend by growing back together.

New **blood cells** are made inside the bigger bones in your body.

You have **206** bones in all. As a baby you had around **300**, but some join together as you grow.

Mysterious Brain

Your brain is your onboard computer. It controls everything from your thoughts and feelings to breathing and eating. Let's peer inside and find out more....

Every day your brain soaks up lessons and experiences. It uses them to help solve new problems.

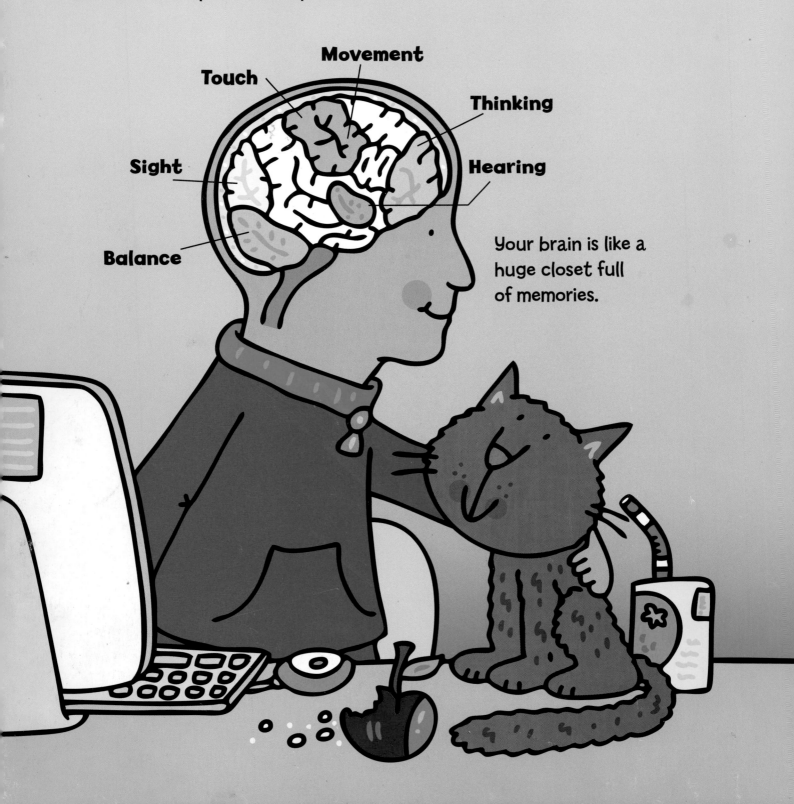

Touch

Movement

Thinking

Sight

Hearing

Balance

Your brain is like a huge closet full of memories.

The brain has **two halves**. Each controls the opposite side of the body. Some jobs, like breathing, are done automatically, which means you don't have to think about it!

Nerves are thin strings that run from your brain through your body. They carry messages to and from your brain.

The more often you do a task, the easier your brain finds it.

FUN FACTS

Did You Know?
An adult brain is a similar weight to a 1.5 quart (1.5 liter) bottle of water.

Sleep is important. It helps the brain to rest. After several days without sleep, the brain does very odd things, like seeing things that aren't really there!

WOW!

Your brain can send messages at speeds faster than a racing car!

Super Senses

All day your eyes, ears, nose, skin, and tongue work overtime to let you know what the world outside your body looks, sounds, smells, feels, and tastes like.

Your **ears** are like microphones picking up all the sounds around you.

Your **nose** can detect more than 10,000 different smells.

Sensors in your skin can feel even the lightest touch, how hard you are pressing against something, and heat and pain.

Did You Know?
Children have sharper hearing than adults and can hear more high-pitched sounds.

Your tongue can detect five tastes – sweet, sour, salty, bitter, and savory flavor.

WOW!

Smell and memory are linked – smelling something can remind you of an event or place.

Ah! Great goal!

Bumps on your **tongue** work with smell to help you taste nice and nasty flavors.

Optical illusions fool your **brain.** Believe it or not, these red lines are straight!

Your awesome **eyes** are video cameras, sending a stream of information to your brain about the world around you.

Going Boom Boom!

No matter how quiet it is, you can always hear something - the sound of your heart thumping and blood sloshing around your pipes.

Blood carries everything your body needs. It gets food and oxygen to all parts, and helps keep you germ-free.

Your **heart** is about the same size as your clenched fist. Over a lifetime your heart pumps the equivalent of 120 Olympic-sized swimming pools of blood!

If the **blood vessels** in your body were laid out end to end, they would loop more than twice around Earth!

When you exercise, your **heart** pumps harder and faster to get more blood to your **muscles**.

Your **lungs** work harder, too, as your muscles need more oxygen.

Your **lungs** gulp down air; they suck up vital oxygen and blow out waste carbon dioxide. Spread out flat they would cover a tennis court!

What Happens to My Food?

Food is the fuel your body works on. But first your meals must go on a roller-coaster ride through your body, all the way from your mouth to your rear end.

The journey begins when your **mouth** mushes food into a gooey lump that you swallow.

The food is squirted into your **intestines**, which are almost as long as a bus!

When food hits your **stomach**, it is broken down into smaller parts by acid. The acid is strong enough to dissolve metal!

In your guts the good stuff, or **nutrients**, is taken out of the food and used by your body as fuel.

Did You Know?
When you swallow, it takes just 10 seconds for food to reach your stomach.

Ready..Steady...Go!

It takes about six hours for your body to process a meal.

WOW!

Over your lifetime, you will produce enough spit to fill a swimming pool!

Poops, Pees, and More

PAAARP! Oops, excuse me! Like poops and pees, burps and
farts are a fact of life. Everyone does 'em - even your teacher.
But why do we do these things?

Burps are made of
similar stuff to farts,
but come out of
your mouth!

Tiny bacteria live in our guts
and help us to digest food.
They release **gases** that pop out...
usually when you least want them to!

Top 3 Gassy Foods:

No.3
Brussels Sprouts

No.2
Fizzy Drinks

No.1
Baked Beans

Your **kidneys** make pee, or urine, which is the liquid waste from your body. It trickles into your **bladder** until you really need to go!

Kidneys

Bladder

Rectum

Poop, or **feces**, is all the bits of food that your body can't digest. About a third of your poop is bacteria. Yuck!

Getting Sick

Your body is always under attack from tiny germs - bugs far too small to see without a microscope - and sometimes they can make you really sick.

Some germs, called **bacteria**, cause stomach upsets and sore throats.

Others, called **viruses,** cause snotty colds, fevers, and flu.

When you are ill, your body fights back by raising its **temperature** so the germs can't survive.

When you sneeze, 40,000 germy droplets spray everywhere. This is how a **cold** spreads between people.

When you've eaten something bad, or your body detects germy invaders, your belly pushes its "**EJECT**" button and you vomit.

Up comes your meal, along with whatever your body is trying to get rid of.

If germs survive your stomach acid, the body gets rid of them with a bout of **diarrhea**, or "the runs"!

Did You Know?

Stand back! The record for "projectile vomiting" is 30 feet (9 meters) – the length of an average school bus.

The ancient Egyptians used animal poop to treat some illnesses!

WOW!

You may suffer as many as 200 colds in a lifetime.

Take Care!

Bathing and brushing your teeth might seem like a drag, but if you want to feel good and grow up strong, you have to follow some very simple basics.

The number one rule is to eat **healthy foods** such as fruit and vegetables and drink plenty of **water**.

Your superstrong **skin** keeps you cool and repairs itself. Look after it by keeping clean!

The more you use your **muscles,** the stronger and springier they become.

Avoid too much fatty, sweet, and salty food - just have a little now and then as a treat.

Bacteria rots your teeth and gives you bad breath. Brush your teeth twice a day to keep bacteria at bay!

Greasy, lanky **hair** isn't nice. Treat it to a shampoo once in a while!

If you don't wash regularly, you'll start to **stink**! Bathing or showering gets rid of dirt and germs.

Amazing Body Facts

You spend about half an hour a day **blinking**.

Everyone's left lung is slightly **smaller** than their right one.

You can't **sneeze** when you're asleep.

The smallest muscle in the body is called the **stapedius**. It's just one-twentieth of an inch (1.25 mm) long and is found in the ear.

There are more **bacteria** in the mouth than there are people on Earth!

The **loudest** snore on record roared in at 80 decibels – that's as noisy as a jackhammer.

World Beaters

The world's **tallest** man is Sultan Kosen of Turkey – a skyscraping 8 feet 1 inch (2.5 m).

Pingping, from Mongolia, was the world's **smallest** man, measuring just 29.3 inches (74.4 cm).

The **oldest** human on record was Frenchwoman Jeanne Calment, who lived for 122 years and 164 days.

Amazing stretch-face Gary Turner from the UK managed to clamp a record-breaking **159 clothes pegs** to his face!

Radhakant Bajpai, from India, has the world's **hairiest** ears. His ear tufts are a tickly 5.2 inches (13.2 cm) long.